Tanya *the* Chicken

Other fun books from Orchard:

Potion Commotion
Jonathan Allen

Fizzy Hits the Headlines
Michael Coleman

The Scribblers of Scumbagg School
Wes Magee

Tanya the Chicken

SONIA HOLLEYMAN

ORCHARD BOOKS

For Anna, Robyn
and Abby

ORCHARD BOOKS
96 Leonard Street, London EC2A 4RH
ORCHARD BOOKS AUSTRALIA
14 Mars Road, Lane Cove, NSW 2066
1 85213 239 6 (hardback)
1 85213 654 5 (paperback)
First published in Great Britain in 1993
First paperback publication 1994
Text and illustrations © Sonia Holleyman 1993
The right of Sonia Holleyman to be identified as Author of this Work has
been asserted by her in accordance with the Copyright, Designs and
Patents Act, 1988
A CIP catalogue record for this book is available from the British Library
Printed in Great Britain

Contents

Chapter One   7
Colin's Big Day

Chapter Two   25
The Sad Return

Chapter Three   35
Try Try Again

Chapter Four   49
Can Chickens Swim?

It was the day of the country fair and
Colin the cockerel had been entered for
the Best Fowl Award. The animals on
Scallybone Farm were helping him to
get ready.

"Stand still!" snorted Razorback the pig as they combed Colin's feathers. "We can't turn you into a champion if you keep wriggling!"

"It's no good!" Colin wailed. He scratched the earth nervously. "I'm just too tatty to win a prize!"

"Don't be silly," said Derek the duck. "You're looking great!"

Soon it was time to leave. Colin's beak was given one last polish and then he climbed into his crate. His friends gathered round to say goodbye and Blanche the ewe came forward and handed Colin a four-leaf clover.

"For good luck!" she bleated. The friends looked on proudly.

Then Razorback shouted, "Three cheers for Colin!"

"Hip, hip, hurrah!" the farm animals cheered, as Colin was loaded into the farmer's van and driven away. Colin felt like a champion already.

After a long, bumpy ride through the country lanes, the farmer's van eventually arrived at the fair.

"Crikey!" clucked Colin, "this fair is even busier than the farmyard!" He gazed about in amazement. People wandered about among colourful stalls, and looked at the animals who had been entered for the Best of the Fair Awards.

Colin's crate was numbered and then
it was placed with the other competitors
to be inspected by the judges.

"Wowee!" Colin whistled as he admired his handsome rivals. "Look at their silky feathers and bright combs. They're so good-looking!"

The other cockerels were indeed very smart, with magnificent emerald tails and glossy feathers. They strutted proudly around preening themselves.

But they didn't think much of Colin. Instead they rolled about in their crates laughing. "Look here, boys! Have you ever seen such a strange-looking fowl as this one?"

"Oi! Turkey face!" they cried and pointed their wings. Colin cowered in humiliation.

Poor Colin had never felt so out of place. He wished he had never been entered for this stupid competition. He ruffled his green feathers. He was just a loser.

But at that moment another crate was put down next to Colin's. In it was the most beautiful chicken he had ever seen. She had golden feathers and pretty white fluffy bits about her feet.

When the other cockerels saw her, they immediately began to show off.

"Oi! Over here!" they cried rudely. But the beautiful chicken ignored them and turned to Colin.

"Hello," she said. "My name is Tanya and I'm from Fernbrook Farm." She looked at Colin with her sparkling

eyes and asked, "Are you in the competition?"

A huge blush spread across Colin's
beak. He pecked the floor shyly.

"I'm Colin, from Scallybone Farm," he
spluttered. "I don't think I should be
here. I'm such an ordinary cockerel."

But Tanya gave him an encouraging smile. "You don't want to listen to them, Colin. I think you're very special. You could easily win a prize."

The two chickens soon became close friends. Colin told stories about his friends on Scallybone Farm. Tanya, who led a rather lonely life at her farm was envious. "I wish I could meet them all!" she said.

Colin realised he was falling in love with this beautiful and kind chicken, when a pair of hands stuck a large red rosette onto Tanya's crate and picked it up.

"Quick!" she cried, "let's swap feathers, so I can remember you until we meet again!"

Colin clutched his golden feather and watched with tears in his eyes as Tanya was carried away.

"Goodbye, Tanya!" Colin cried. But she had already disappeared.

The Sad Return

It was evening when a miserable Colin returned to Scallybone Farm. All his friends were waiting in the farmyard to greet him.

"How did you get on, Colin? Did you win?" grunted Razorback the pig.

"No," said Colin. "But I won a far greater prize."

He produced Tanya's silken feather. "I've fallen in love!" he said. And he added sadly, "Oh, dear Tanya. But I will never see her again."

Colin told his friends about the unfriendly cockerels and how he met the beautiful, kind Tanya. Razorback and Derek looked on sadly. Blanche wiped a tear from her eye. She realised that a prize-winning chicken like Tanya would never be allowed to leave Fernbrook Farm again.

Then Derek (who was normally quite a dim duck) had a brilliant idea.

"Why don't you go and get Tanya?" he asked.

"Of course!" cried Blanche, bleating excitedly. "You could fly in and rescue her. How exciting!"

The animals started skipping round the yard flapping their legs happily. But Colin looked at the ground in embarrassment.

"But I can't fly," he said.

"Don't be daft," snorted Razorback the pig. "You've got wings. If Derek can fly so can you!"

Soon after this Colin stood on the hayloft roof. Derek was enjoying himself, giving advice and lots of useful tips.

"Point your feet at the ground and quack!" he said.

"This will never work," said Colin. "I know I can't fly. I think I'll – "

A small pair of trotters pushed him from behind. Colin closed his eyes as he felt himself falling.

"Flap!" honked Razorback.

"Flap!" bleated Blanche.

"Flap, Colin, flap!" shouted the others.

But it was no good. Colin landed with a thump in the farmyard.

"I told you!" Colin cried. "I'm just a loser."

Blanche scratched her head thoughtfully. "Perhaps he'd fly better with duck's feathers?" she said.

The animals all looked at Derek, who backed off slowly ...

Try Try Again

After some minor adjustments, Colin soon found himself back on the hayloft roof. He felt really stupid with Derek's feathers stuck all over him. He peeked over the edge. His friends looked much smaller from up here.

Fly for Tanya!

"Fly, Colin, fly!" they shouted up from down below. "Fly for Tanya!"

Colin took a deep breath, stepped off the roof and launched himself into the air. Flapping with all his might, he fell like a stone to the ground below.

At that moment a loud buzzing filled the air. The animals looked up at the sky.

"A flying machine!" cried Razorback and he waved his trotters excitedly. "Of course! If Colin can't fly alone, we'll build him a machine to fly in."

Razorback soon had them all orga-
nised, and the animals went off to find
as many useful things as they could.

Blanche came back with a small
bundle of sticks, and her lamb had bor-
rowed a very nice balloon.

39

Razorback went straight to the rubbish bin (his favourite place) and found a very nice tin can. It was covered in crusty baked beans which he was able to lick off.

Dotty the old cart horse had just finished work and she agreed to help the
search party. She remembered seeing a
rusty umbrella out in the field she was
ploughing, and she went off to collect it.

Derek couldn't find anything, so he gave the rest of his best feathers.

It wasn't long before they had a large collection of things. Razorback arranged the bits on the yard floor, and the animals set to work.

Colin was getting over-excited at the thought of flying in his machine to Tanya. So Blanche sent him off to his coop to pack his things.

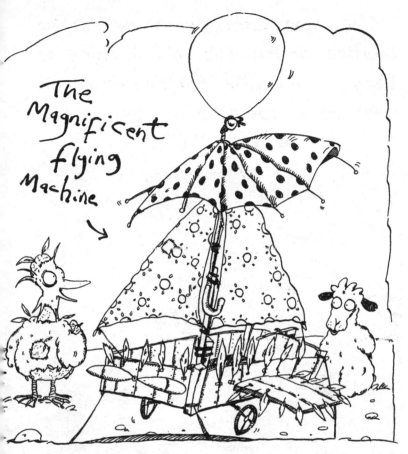

The Magnificent flying Machine →

The animals were up all night but by morning they had finished. There, in the yard, stood the most magnificent flying machine ever seen.

"It's amazing!" said Colin, as he climbed aboard. He stowed away his luggage, his packed lunch and his lucky wellington boot (which Razorback had also found in the dustbin).

Dotty, who had once been to Fern-brook Farm, had drawn a map to help Colin find his way. Colin pinned it to the mast.

"I told you we would get you flying!" Razorback honked proudly, as Colin waved goodbye to his friends.

Razorback set the cogs, wheels and spinny things in motion and ceremoniously cut the anchor ropes.

Colin and his flying machine gracefully drifted into the morning air. He was on his way to Tanya.

Meanwhile, at Fernbrook Farm, a sad and lonely Tanya sat dreaming of her Colin. Little did she know that he was risking his neck for her at that very moment.

Green slimy Pond

The journey was going well and Colin had decided that flying was a piece of cake. Who needed wings when you had a magnificent flying machine?

But then, halfway across a green slimy pond, he suddenly realised he was losing height. He wasn't even sure if chickens could swim.

"I'm going to drown!" Colin sobbed as the machine sank lower ... and lower.

But just as he was losing all hope, Colin
saw Fernbrook Farm in the distance.

"Tanya, here I come!" he cried,
jumping up and down in excitement.
The machine rocked dangerously.

Tanya was scratching away in the farmyard when she spotted the machine. She couldn't believe her eyes. Was it really her Colin appearing on the horizon?

...Was it really her Colin?

"I'm here!" Tanya cried, leaping for joy, and she raced towards the flying machine. Colin lowered the string ladder and began to pull her up.

When Tanya was safely on board they rushed into each other's wings and hugged excitedly.

"Oh, Colin," Tanya cried, "I never thought I'd see you again!"

Colin turned his machine round, and the happy chickens began to float back towards Scallybone Farm.

But the machine was much too heavy
with two chickens on board and it began
to sink back down to earth.

"We're going to crash!" Colin wailed
and he covered his eyes with his wings.

Luckily Tanya was a sensible chicken.
"We've got to make the machine

lighter!" she cried. "If we throw everything overboard, it won't sink so
quickly." And with that she picked up
Colin's lucky wellington boot and threw
it overboard.

Colin helped Tanya strip the machine
bare and toss everything away.

Very slowly, and much to the relief of the two friends, the machine rose a little higher and inched its way homewards.

As they drew near the farm, Colin told Tanya how his good friends had helped him save her. How Derek the duck had given away his best feathers and how Razorback had masterminded the whole thing. Tanya promised not to laugh when she saw poor bald Derek.

Soon Scallybone Farm appeared on the horizon. "There it is!" cried Colin. "There's the farm. Razorback, Blanche, and all my friends will be waiting for us!"

Colin and Tanya hung on to each other tightly as the machine bumped along the ground and came to a triumphant halt inside the farmyard.

Tanya helped Colin out of the machine. Together they stood and looked around the deserted farmyard. Colin's friends were nowhere to be seen.

"Razorback, Blanche, Derek!" Colin called. "We're home!" But all was quiet. Tanya sat down and ruffled her feathers.

Then, suddenly, with a huge cheer, the barn doors flew open and out jumped Derek, Blanche, Razorback and all the other farm animals.

"Three cheers for Colin and Tanya!" they cried. "Hurrah, hurrah, hurrah!"

They all gathered round and were introduced to Tanya, who took them in her wings and thanked them all for their help.

Then Razorback led Colin, Tanya and all the farm animals into the barn, where Blanche and her lamb had prepared a Welcome Home feast.

Then they all settled down to hear about the great adventure of two brave chickens, which was sure to go down in history.

When the stories and the cheers were over, they had a party that continued deep into the night.

Here are Sonia Holleyman and her cat
Oscar. Oscar writes and illustrates the
books and Sonia is his assistant. They
both live in Essex.